C000228300

מסורה

ArtScroll Youth Series ®

The Children's Book of

by
David A. Adler

illustrated by
Dovid Sears

Jewish Holidays

Published by

Mesorah Publications, ltd

FIRST EDITION
First Impression . . . November, 1987
Second Impression . . . December, 1989
Third Impression . . . October, 1991
Fourth Impression . . . August 1996
Fifth Impression . . . December 1999

Published and Distributed by
MESORAH PUBLICATIONS, Ltd.
4401 Second Avenue
Brooklyn, New York 11232

Distributed in Europe by
J. LEHMANN HEBREW BOOKSELLERS
20 Cambridge Terrace
Gateshead, Tyne and Wear
England NE8 1RP

Distributed in Israel by
SIFRIATI / A. GITLER — BOOKS
10 Hashomer Street
Bnei Brak 51361

Distributed in Australia & New Zealand by
GOLDS BOOK & GIFT CO.
36 William Street
Balaclava 3183, Vic., Australia

Distributed in South Africa by
KOLLEL BOOKSHOP
Shop 8A Norwood Hypermarket
Norwood 2196, Johannesburg, South Africa

ARTSCROLL YOUTH SERIES®
THE CHILDREN'S BOOK OF JEWISH HOLIDAYS
© *Copyright 1987, 1996, by* MESORAH PUBLICATIONS, Ltd.
4401 Second Avenue / Brooklyn, N.Y. 11232 / (718) 921-9000

No part of this book may be reproduced
in any form — **including photocopying and retrieval systems** —
without **written** *permission from the copyright holder,*
except by a reviewer who wishes to quote brief passages in connection with a review
written for inclusion in magazines or newspapers.

THE RIGHTS OF THE COPYRIGHT HOLDER WILL BE STRICTLY ENFORCED.

ISBN:
0-89906-810-3 (hard cover)
0-89906-811-1 (paperback)

Typography by CompuScribe at ArtScroll Studios, Ltd.
4401 Second Avenue / Brooklyn, N.Y. 11232 / (718) 921-9000

Printed in the United States of America by Maven Quality Printers
Bound by Sefercraft Inc., Quality Bookbinders, Brooklyn, N.Y.

Table of Contents

The Jewish Calendar

e have our own calendar. But unlike the general calendar which is based on the sun, ours is based on the moon. We celebrate our holidays on the same Jewish dates each year. For example, *Pesach* (Passover) always begins on the fifteenth day of the Hebrew month of Nissan. But while it's always celebrated in the spring, the date in the general calendar for the first day of *Pesach* changes from year to year. It can begin as early as the end of March or as late as the last week in April.

The Jewish Calendar year is divided into twelve months. During leap years there are thirteen. Leap years come seven times every nineteen years.

The Jewish New Year begins on the first day of the Hebrew month of *Tishrei*. *Tishrei* and the two months which follow, *Cheshvan* and *Kislev*, are in the autumn. *Teves, Shevat* and *Adar* are winter months. During a leap year a month is added, *Adar Sheni*. It falls between the end of winter and the beginning of spring. *Nissan, Iyar* and *Sivan* are spring months. *Tammuz, Av* and *Elul* are summer months.

Shabbos — The Sabbath

ach Friday afternoon, as the sun is about to set, we welcome *Shabbos,* the day of rest. Through the generations Jews have loved *Shabbos* and have called it a "taste of the World to Come." It's a day of study, prayer and peace.

The fourth of the Ten Commandments tells us, "Remember the day of *Shabbos* to make it holy. For six days you shall labor and do all your work. But the seventh is a Sabbath of the L-rd, your G-d. You may not do any work, neither you, your son, your daughter, your man servants, your maid servants, your animals nor the stranger who lives among you. Because in six days the L-rd made the heavens, the earth, the sea, and all that is in them, and He rested on the seventh day. That is why the L-rd blessed the day of *Shabbos* and made it holy."

On *Shabbos* we do not work. We don't write, bake, build, light a fire or do any other of the thirty-nine types of work done to build the Temple. During *Shabbos* we don't even move tools used for such work.

We light candles in our homes before sunset on Friday to welcome *Shabbos.*

On Friday night before *Maariv* in the synagogue, we say six psalms, one for each of the regular days of the week. Then we welcome the *Shabbos* Queen by singing *Lechah Dodi* and reciting two special psalms.

Before we eat on Friday night and *Shabbos* morning we hold a cup of wine and say *Kiddush,* a blessing for the *Shabbos.* In *Kiddush* we recall that G-d created the world in six days and rested on the seventh. And we recall that G-d took the Jewish people out of Egypt and made us into a nation.

On *Shabbos* we eat three meals — one on Friday night, one after synagogue services in the morning, and one before sunset. We eat fish, meat and all sorts of delicious food. At each meal we eat *challah,* a tasty white bread baked especially for *Shabbos* and holidays. And we sing *zemiros,* songs which praise G-d and *Shabbos.*

Every *Shabbos* morning in the synagogue, a different portion of the Torah is read. During the course of the year, beginning with the first *Shabbos* following *Simchas Torah,* the entire Five Books of Moses are read. And following the Torah reading on *Shabbos*, the *Haftarah,* a chapter from *Nevi'im,* the Prophets, is read.

After dark on Saturday, we say *Havdalah,* the prayer which separates *Shabbos* from the other days in the week. *Havdalah* is said over wine, spices and candlelight.

Rosh Hashanah
— The Jewish New Year

osh Hashanah is the Jewish New Year. It is celebrated on the first two days of the Hebrew month of *Tishrei.* It's a holiday of great beginnings, of judgment and of *shofar* blowing.

The first great beginning was the Creation of the world. According to Rabbi Eliezer, the Six Days of Creation were completed on the first of *Tishrei,* with the creation of Adam and Eve. On the first of *Tishrei,* Abraham and Jacob were born. G-d remembered Sarah, Rachel and Hannah on the first of *Tishrei* and blessed them with children. Joseph was freed from prison. And the Jews stopped working as slaves in Egypt. It is a day of great beginnings.

Rosh Hashanah is the Day of Judgment. On it, all people pass before G-d. He reviews our deeds of the past year, and decides our fate for the coming year. G-d decides ''who will be at rest and who will wander, who will have an easy year and who will have a hard year, who will live in peace and who will suffer, who will become poor and who will become rich.''

In order to prepare for the Day of Judgment, we blow a *shofar*, ram's horn, each day for a month before *Rosh Hashanah.* The sounds should awaken us to remember our

deeds and to do *teshuvah,* to repent, to feel sorry for our misdeeds and to try our best not to repeat them.

During the week before *Rosh Hashanah,* prayers of repentance, called *Selichos,* are said each morning. In these prayers we ask G-d to forgive our sins of the past and we promise to be better in the future.

We also ask our friends and relatives — especially if we have quarreled with them — to forgive us if we have treated them badly during the year.

Many Jews have the custom on *Rosh Hashanah* to eat round *challah.* At dinner on the two nights of the holiday, we dip the *challah* and a slice of apple into honey and ask G-d to give us all a good and sweet year. Many families use round *challos* each *Shabbos* and holiday from *Rosh Hashanah* until the end of *Succos* (Tabernacles).

The *shofar* is blown one hundred times during the morning services on each day of *Rosh Hashanah* (but not if *Rosh Hashanah* is on *Shabbos*).

In the afternoon of the first day of *Rosh Hashanah,* a special prayer, *Tashlich,* is said near a body of water. In it we remember how G-d has forgiven our sins in past years. We pray that He will again forgive us. It is our hope that our sins will be removed from us as if they were swallowed by the sea.

The ten days beginning with *Rosh Hashanah* and ending with *Yom Kippur* are called the Ten days of Repentance. These days are set aside for *teshuvah.* Each weekday morning we recite *Selichos.* We are extra careful about doing the *mitzvos.* And we give more charity than usual.

Yom Kippur
— The Day of Atonement

om Kippur, the tenth of *Tishrei,* is a day of thought, prayer and fasting. It is the day set aside in the Torah for *teshuvah,* repentance and return to G-d. On this day we pray for all our sins to be forgiven.

For the entire day of *Yom Kippur,* men and women, boys past thirteen and girls past twelve, do not eat or drink. We do not wear leather shoes, or bathe, or put on perfumes and lotions. In the synagogue, men wear a *kittel,* an all-white robe, to be like the white-clothed angels of G-d.

We say *vidui* many times to confess our sins. In the *vidui,* sixty-six sins are listed, three for each letter of the Hebrew alphabet. We stand and gently hit our chests each time we name a sin. And even if there are sins in the *vidui* which we surely did not do, we still name them, because we are praying for others as well as ourselves.

We say our first *vidui* during the *Minchah* prayer just before we eat the last meal before *Yom Kippur.* The last *vidui* is during the *Ne'ilah* prayer at the very end of *Yom Kippur.*

The *Avodah* prayer is said during *Mussaf.* In this prayer we recall the service that the *Kohen Gadol* performed in the *Beis Hamikdash,* the Temple. We pray that the *Beis*

Hamikdash be restored and that we will be able to take part in the services there.

The book of Jonah is read during *Minchah,* the afternoon prayer. G-d told Jonah about the wicked people living in the city of Nineveh. He told Jonah to go to Nineveh and to teach the people to stop their evil ways, to do *teshuvah.* But Jonah did not want to go. He tried to run away from G-d. He went aboard a boat headed for Tarshish. At sea a great storm threatened to split the boat apart. Jonah knew the storm was because of him so he asked to be thrown overboard. As soon as he was off the boat, the storm stopped. Jonah was swallowed by a fish so large that he was able to live in it. Inside that fish, Jonah prayed to G-d and was forgiven. The fish brought Jonah ashore and Jonah went to Nineveh as G-d had told him to do. There he preached to the people and told them to repent. They stopped their evil deeds, and they too were forgiven. We pray on *Yom Kippur* that we will also be forgiven.

At the end of *Yom Kippur* the *shofar* is blown once. Then we pray that next year we will all be together, a united people in a rebuilt Jerusalem.

Succos — Tabernacles

On the fifteenth of *Tishrei*, five days after *Yom Kippur*, the joyous holiday of *Succos* begins. We eat in a *succah*, a temporary room. Many sleep in their *succos* too.

The walls of a *succah* are built first. Then the *schach*, the roof of the *succah*, is put on. It may be made only of something which grew from the ground. It should provide more shade than sun. But there should also be enough space between the *schach* so that at night someone sitting in the *succah* could look up and see the stars.

We build a *succah* and eat in it to remember the time the Jews traveled in the Wilderness after G-d brought them out of Egypt. As they traveled they built *succos* to protect themselves from the sun during the day and the cold at night. The *succah* also reminds us of the *Ananai Hakavod*, the *Clouds of Glory* which G-d placed around the Jewish people to protect them during their years in the Wilderness.

Each day of *Succos*, except *Shabbos*, we hold together and shake a *lulav* (the branch of a palm tree), an *esrog* (citron), three *hadassim* (branches of a myrtle bush), and two *aravos* (branches of a willow tree). We shake them while reciting the *Hallel* prayers and we walk with them around the synagogue *bimah*, the table on which the Torah is read. As we walk we say prayers. And after each verse of these prayers we say, "*Hoshana* — please save us."

Our Sages taught that these four species represent the

Jewish people. The *esrog* has a good taste as well as a pleasant smell. And there are Jews who study G-d's Torah and do good deeds.

The palm tree from which a *lulav* is taken has dates, a fruit with a good taste. But the palm tree has no smell. And there are Jews with learning but without good deeds.

The *hadassim* have a pleasant smell but no taste. And there are Jews who do good deeds but are without learning.

The *aravos* have no smell and no taste. And there are Jews without learning and without good deeds.

During *Succos* we hold all four species together. And the Jewish people should all work together, helping one another and each one learning Torah and good deeds from the other.

In the Land of Israel the first day of *Succos* is a holiday when no work is done. Outside the Land of Israel no work is done during the first two days of *Succos.* The remaining days are called *Chol Hamoed, the* intermediate days. These days are semi-holidays.

During the *Shabbos* of *Succos* the book of *Koheles* (Ecclesiastes) is read. In it King Solomon writes that it is foolish to continually want to buy more and own more. We should instead want to do more, more of G-d's commandments.

The seventh day of *Succos* is *Hoshana Rabbah.* We say special prayers and carry our *lulav, esrog, hadassim* and *aravos* as we walk seven times around the *bimah.* At the end of the *Hoshana* prayers, we hold five *aravos* which are tied together and beat them on the floor. Our Sages teach that on *Succos* G-d decides how much rain will fall during the year ahead. *Aravos* are symbols of rain because willow trees, from which *aravos* are cut, usually grow alongside a body of water.

Shemini Atzeres and Simchas Torah

hemini Atzeres is celebrated on the twenty-second of *Tishrei,* right after the seven days of *Succos.* But it's a separate holiday and, as on the first days of *Succos,* work may not be done on it. Why does it follow *Succos*? Our rabbis teach us that just as a parent does not want his children to leave at the end of a visit, G-d does not want His people to leave at the end of *Succos.* So He gave us the holiday of *Shemini Atzeres.*

We say a special prayer for rain on *Shemini Atzeres.* We also add four words to our daily prayers, מַשִּׁיב הָרוּחַ וּמוֹרִיד הַגֶּשֶׁם, saying that G-d causes the wind to blow and the rain to fall. We will continue to say these four words until the first day of *Pesach,* when heavy rains are no longer a blessing in the Land of Israel.

Simchas Torah is a Torah celebration. Outside the Land of Israel it is celebrated on the twenty-third of *Tishrei,* the day following *Shimini Atzeres.* But in the Land of Israel, *Shemini Atzeres* and *Simchas Torah* are celebrated on the same day, the twenty-second of *Tishrei.*

Each *Shabbos* we read a portion of the Torah, the Five Books of Moses. We read in order, one portion after another, from the first portion, *Bereishis,* until the last, *Vezos Haberachah.* On *Simchas Torah* we complete the

reading of the Torah, and then we go back to the beginning of the Torah and start to read *Bereishis* again.

On the night of *Simchas Torah* and in the morning all the Torah scrolls are taken from the Ark. We sing and dance with them. We carry the Torah scrolls in a circle at least seven times around the *bimah*, the table on which the Torah is read. During the morning of *Simchas Torah* it is the custom that every man and boy, even the very young, is called to the Torah and makes a blessing.

When the Torah scrolls are all taken from the Ark it is the custom in some synagogues to put a lighted candle into the Ark. This reminds us that the light of the Torah is found there.

Chanukah

*C*hanukah is celebrated for eight days beginning with the twenty-fifth of Kislev. It celebrates our great victory over the powerful Syrian-Greek armies and the miracle of a small jar of oil.

During the time of the Second Temple, King Antiochus the Fourth of Syria ruled over the land of Israel. He stole from the Jews and sold some as slaves. He stole from the Temple. He brought a Greek idol into the Temple and forced Jews to bow to it. Any Jew who refused was killed. Any Jew who observed *Shabbos,* kept *Rosh Chodesh,* studied the Torah or circumcised his son was killed, too.

The king's soldiers placed idols throughout the Land of Israel. In the town of Modiin they set up an idol and tried to force an old man, Mattisyahu, to bow to it. He refused. And when another man was about to bow to the idol, Mattisyahu struck the man down and called out, "Whoever is for the L-rd, our G-d, follow me!"

Mattisyahu, his five sons and their followers ran to the hills. They hid there and fought the powerful armies of the king. Antiochus sent his best generals and soldiers against the small group of fighting Jews. The Greek soldiers came with swords, bows, arrows and even elephants covered with armor. The Jews were led by Mattisyahu. After he died his son Yehudah Hamaccabee became the leader. They fought off the armies of Antiochus and re-entered the Temple in Jerusalem.

The Temple was overgrown with vines and weeds, filled with garbage, and on the Altar was an idol. The Jews cleaned the Temple. But when they were ready to light the *Menorah* in the Temple, they could find only one small jar of oil with the seal of the *Kohen Gadol.* There was enough oil in that jar to burn just one day. But that oil burned and burned for eight days and nights until more oil could be prepared.

During the eight nights of *Chanukah* we remember that miracle by lighting the *Menorah* in our homes and synagogues. We use either oil lamps or candles. We begin with one light the first night. We add one each night until the last night of *Chanukah* when eight lights are lit.

We recite the blessings, kindle the lights and sing *Haneros Halalu* as we recall the miracles of *Chanukah*. We also sing *Ma'oz Tzur* in which we thank G-d for all the times He has saved us from our enemies.

The *Chanukah* lights also symbolize the light of Torah. Many nations have tried to snuff out the study of Torah, but we remain loyal to the Torah and keep its light shining brightly.

On *Chanukah* we eat *latkes* (potato pancakes), and *sufganiyot* (doughnuts). Both are made with oil and remind us of the small jar of oil that burned and burned. We also play with a *dreidel,* a four-sided spinning top. On each side of the *dreidel* is a Hebrew letter reminding us of the *Chanukah* miracle. Outside the Land of Israel the letters are נ ג ה ש which stand for the words, נֵס גָּדוֹל הָיָה שָׁם, a great miracle happened there. In the Land of Israel the four letters on the *dreidel* are נ ג ה פ which stand for the words, נֵס גָּדוֹל הָיָה פֹּה, a great miracle happened here.

Tu BiShvat

Tu BiShvat, the fifteenth day of *Shevat,* is the New Year for trees. In many countries it seems strange to celebrate the rebirth of trees in the middle of winter. But in the Land of Israel the rainy season has just ended and buds are beginning to appear on the trees.

We eat fruits and nuts on *Tu BiShvat.* We especially try to eat the fruits for which the Torah praises the Land of Israel. The Torah describes the Land of Israel as a good land, "a land of . . . vines, figs, and pomegranates . . . olives and sweet dates." So on *Tu BiShvat* we eat grapes, figs, pomegranates, olives and dates. We also eat fruit that we haven't eaten during the year so we can say the blessing *Shehechiyanu.* In that blessing we thank G-d for keeping us alive and healthy as a part of His world until this day.

Some people have the custom to pray on *Tu BiShvat* that G-d provide them with a beautiful, kosher *esrog* for the next year's *Succos* holiday.

Purim

and Ta'anis Esther

n the fourteenth of *Adar,* one month before the beginning of *Pesach*, we celebrate *Purim.* It's an especially joyous holiday.

On the night of *Purim* and in the morning, the Book of Esther, the *Megillah,* is read. It tells the story of *Purim.* When we hear the story, we may not think of it as a miracle. Throughout the *Megillah,* G-d's name is never mentioned. But our Rabbis teach us that the miracles of *Purim* are hidden, made to appear natural. They teach us that G-d's work continues even in seemingly everyday occurrences.

The Book of Esther tells of King Ahasuerus who ruled one hundred and twenty-seven provinces, from India to Ethiopia. He had a beautiful queen. Her name was Vashti. But when Vashti refused to come to the king at a great party he made, the king had her killed. He selected a new queen, Esther. She was a Jew. But neither he nor anyone on his staff knew that she was Jewish.

Haman, a wicked enemy of the Jews, was the king's chief minister. Haman planned to kill every Jew in the empire. The king gave Haman permission to carry out his plans. He signed a decree. On the thirteenth of *Adar* the Jews would be killed.

Esther's uncle Mordechai tore his clothes and cried for his people. And he told Esther what was about to happen. Esther went to the king to beg for her people. The king told her that his first decree could not be changed. But he did give the Jews the right to fight and defend themselves.

The night before Esther asked the king to spare the Jews, Haman went to the king to ask permission to hang Mordechai on gallows Haman had prepared. But that very night King Ahasuerus was reminded that Mordechai had once saved his life. Nothing had been done to reward Mordechai for this. The king told Haman to dress Mordechai in royal clothes, seat him on the king's horse and lead him through town calling out, "This is what is done for the man the king wishes to honor." Later Haman was hanged on the gallows he had prepared for Mordechai.

The Jews in the cities and provinces organized themselves. They fought and defended themselves against their enemies on the thirteenth of *Adar*. And on the fourteenth they celebrated their great victory.

Mordechai was made the king's new chief minister. And the fourteenth of *Adar* was designated a holiday.

On *Purim* when the Book of Esther is read, each time we hear the name Haman, we shake *graggers* (*Purim* noise-makers) to blot out the name of that wicked man.

On *Purim* we send gifts of food to one another. This is called *shalach manos*. And we give charity to the poor. In the afternoon we have a joyous *seudah* (feast). And it's a custom to eat *hamantashen*, three-cornered little cakes filled with poppy seeds or jelly.

∾§ Ta'anis Esther

This fast day, when adults do not eat or drink, is observed on the thirteenth of *Adar,* the day before *Purim.* (In the Jewish law an adult is any male over the age of thirteen and any female over the age of twelve.) On *Ta'anis Esther* we remember that when the Jews learned of Haman's plans to destroy our people, they fasted for three days and nights.

Pesach — Passover

he eight day holiday of *Pesach* (seven days in the Land of Israel) begins on the fifteenth of *Nissan.* It's a celebration of freedom.

More than three thousand years ago the Jews were slaves in Egypt. Pharaoh (the Egyptian king) forced them to do hard labor, to make bricks and to build storehouses and great stone walls around the cities of Pithom and Raamses. Slaves who did not work quickly enough were beaten. Some were killed. And one day Pharaoh declared that every Jewish boy born should be thrown into the river and drowned.

But one Jewish boy was saved. His mother made a tiny ark for him out of reeds, tar and mud. She hid the ark in the bulrushes, along the edge of the river. The boy was Moses, and years later G-d chose him to lead the Jewish people out of Egypt.

G-d spoke to Moses from the midst of a burning bush. G-d would take the Jews out of Egypt and Moses would be their leader.

G-d sent Moses and his brother Aaron to Pharaoh to free the Jews from slavery. Pharaoh refused. Moses warned him that G-d would turn all of the water in the Nile River and throughout Egypt to blood. Pharaoh still refused. So the water turned to blood. The fish died and there was a terrible odor throughout the land of Egypt. That was the first of ten plagues which G-d brought upon Egypt.

Pharaoh refused again and again to let the Jews go free. After the blood in the river turned back to water, frogs covered the land. Then lice and later wild animals attacked Egypt. The Egyptians' animals were attacked by a deadly disease. Boils broke out on the Egyptians' skin. Large hailstones fell on the land. Hungry locusts ate every growing plant. Later Egypt was wrapped in darkness.

Then, G-d told Moses and Aaron to tell the Jewish people that on the fourteenth day of Nissan each family should slaughter a lamb or a baby goat and place its blood on their doorposts. They should roast the meat and eat it that night with *matzah* and *maror* (bitter herbs).

At midnight, the last plague came. The firstborn son in every Egyptian household died. But the firstborn sons of the Jewish households, those with blood on their doorposts, lived.

Pharaoh told Moses and Aaron that the Jews could go free. They left Egypt early in the morning. They left in such a hurry that there was no time for their dough to rise. Instead of the fluffy bread, it was *matzah.*

Pharaoh and an army of soldiers, horses and chariots chased after them. The Jews ran toward the Sea of Reeds. When they reached it, G-d told Moses to hold his arm over the sea. He did and the waters parted. The Jews walked through on dry land. The Egyptians followed. Moses lifted his arm again and the waters flooded together. Pharaoh's army was drowned. The Jews were free.

Before *Pesach* we rid our homes of all breads, cakes and other *chametz*. We will eat no *chametz* for the eight days of *Pesach* (seven days in the Land of Israel). The first two days and the last two days we do not work (only the first and last day in the Land of Israel). The middle days are called *Chol Hamoed.* They are semi-holidays.

On the first two nights of *Pesach* (but just on the first night in the Land of Israel), we have a special *Seder* meal. At the *Seder* we read the *Haggadah*, which tells about all the miracles G-d did when He brought our people out of Egypt. We eat *matzah* and remember the *matzah* the Jews ate as they left Egypt. We eat *maror*, bitter herbs, and remember the bitter taste of slavery. We dip the *maror* into *charoses*, a mixture that looks like clay, and remember the clay and bricks the slaves used. We drink four cups of wine, and we celebrate our freedom.

Near the beginning of the *Seder*, is the *Mah Nishtanah*, the *Four Questions*, which are asked by the youngest person at the *Seder* who is able to ask. The *Mah Nishtanah* begins with the question, "Why is this night different from all other nights?" The answer, of course, is the history of the Jews in Egypt and how G-d set us free.

The Omer
and Lag B'Omer

eginning with the second night of *Pesach* we count days from the holiday celebrating leaving slavery in Egypt to the holiday celebrating receiving the Torah. The seven weeks of counting are called *Sefirah* which is Hebrew for counting.

Since this counting begins on the second day of *Pesach*, the same day the *Omer* (barley offering) was brought to the Temple, the counting is called "counting the *Omer*".

We count, "Today is one day in the *Omer.*"

"Today is two days in the *Omer.*"

We continue counting until we reach the forty-ninth day, the end of seven weeks. The day after the forty-ninth day in the *Omer* is the holiday of *Shavuos.*

These seven weeks later became a time of mourning, because of the tragedies which occured during these days. Twenty-four thousand students of Rabbi Akiva died in a plague during the days between *Pesach* and *Shavuos.* They were punished because they did not treat each other with proper respect. This should be an important lesson to us. We must always act kindly and respectfully to others.

A thousand years later, during the Crusades in France and Germany, whole communities of Jews were killed

during this *Omer* period. And in the years 1648 and 1649 Bogdan Chmielnicki led Russian Cossacks in the attack and murder of three hundred thousand Jews.

But on the thirty-third day of the *Omer* there is no mourning. The plague which was killing so many of Rabbi Akiva's students stopped on that day. The number thirty-three in Hebrew is written ל"ג which is pronounced *Lag,* and so the day is called *Lag B'Omer.*

Another famous event happened on the eighteenth of *Iyar,* the thirty-third day of the *Omer.* On that day Rabbi Shimon bar Yochai died. He was a great rabbi and teacher. On the day of Rabbi Shimon Bar Yochai's death he taught his students many of the Torah's hidden lessons. On that day the sun did not set, the day did not end, until he had taught them all that G-d allowed him to reveal.

Usually the death of a great man is a day of mourning. But Rabbi Shimon bar Yochai wanted it to be a day of celebration, not mourning. He made this wish because of all the Torah he had been able to teach on that day.

During Rabbi Shimon bar Yochai's lifetime, no rainbow was ever seen in the sky. The Torah tells us that a rainbow is a sign of G-d's anger at man's sins. But while Rabbi Shimon bar Yochai was alive, his many good deeds kept G-d from being angry at the sins of his generation. On *Lag B'Omer* children play with toy bows and arrows to remember the rainbow, which appeared on the day of Rabbi Shimon bar Yochai's death.

The bow and arrow also remind us of another time. When the Romans ruled over the Land of Israel they did not allow Torah study. Anyone caught studying the Torah was killed. Rabbi Akiva did not stop teaching Torah. He said, "Jews without Torah are like fish without water! We must continue studying the Torah!" He and his students disguised themselves as hunters. They carried bows and arrows deep into the woods. There they would study Torah, sometimes while hiding in caves.

In many communities very young boys whose hair has never been cut and who have reached the age of three get their first haircuts on *Lag B'Omer.* In the Land of Israel many people bring their children to Meron, the place where Rabbi Shimon bar Yochai is buried, and there cut their children's hair for the first time. Many thousands of people come to Meron to celebrate Rabbi Shimon bar Yochai's day.

Shavuos

The two day holiday of *Shavuos* (one day in the Land of Israel) begins on the sixth of *Sivan.* It celebrates the day G-d gave us the Torah at *Har Sinai.* For this reason *Shavuos* is also called *Zeman Matan Toraseinu,* the time our Torah was given.

Each year on *Shavuos* we once again accept the Torah, just as we did at *Har Sinai.* Many Jews show how eager they are to receive G-d's Torah by staying up the entire first night of *Shavuos* studying the Torah.

On *Shavuos* it is a custom to eat dairy foods — milk, blintzes and cheesecakes — because the Torah is like milk and honey. And when the number value of each of the letters in the word חָלָב (*chalav,* Hebrew for milk) are added together they equal forty (ח $= 8$; ל $= 30$; and ב $= 2$; for a total of 40). Forty is the number of days Moses was on *Har Sinai* when he received the Torah.

In some communities there was a custom to begin teaching Torah to very young children early on the morning of *Shavuos.* The child's first teacher read the Hebrew letters and the child repeated them. Then the teacher spread honey over the written letters and the child licked the honey off, for the taste of Torah is sweet.

For *Shavuos* we decorate our homes and synagogues with greens and flowers. This is done to remind us of *Har*

Sinai, which was covered with grass and sweet-smelling flowers when G-d gave the Torah.

The name *Shavuos* means "weeks". The holiday comes after counting the *Omer* for seven weeks, a counting which began the second night of *Pesach.*

Shavuos is also called *Atzeres* because together with *Pesach* it forms a unit. We gained our freedom on *Pesach* in order to receive the Torah on *Shavuos.* The weeks of the *Omer* between the two holidays are a link between them, just as *Chol Hamoed* forms a link between *Succos* and *Shemini Atzeres.*

Shavuos has other names, too. It is called *Yom Habikurim,* the Day of the First Fruits, because beginning on *Shavuos* each farmer in the Land of Israel brought to the Temple the first wheat, barley, grapes, figs, pomegranates, olives and dates that grew on his fields.

It is also called *Chag Hakatzir,* the Holiday of the Harvest, because wheat, the last of the grains to be ready to be cut, was harvested at this time of the year.

Tishah B'Av

The ninth day of *Av, Tishah B'Av,* is a day of great sadness and mourning. The first and the second Temples were destroyed on that day.

Many other Jewish tragedies occurred on *Tishah B'Av.* On the eve of *Tishah B'Av* the spies sent by Moses to the Land of Canaan returned to the Jewish camp. They spoke badly of the Land, and they said that the Jews could not defeat the Canaanites in a war. And that night the people wept. It was to become a night of weeping in all generations.

Sixty-five years after the destruction of the Second Temple, the Romans destroyed the city of Betar, where there were hundreds of Torah schools. In 1290, the Jews were chased out of England on the ninth day of *Av.* And in 1492, on *Tishah B'Av,* the Jews were thrown out of Spain.

The mourning for the Temple begins three weeks before *Tishah B'Av* on the seventeenth day of *Tammuz.* On that day, during the time of the Second Temple, the Romans broke through the walls around Jerusalem. During these three weeks we do not cut our hair, wear new clothes, have parties or weddings. During the first nine days of *Av* we do not eat meat or drink wine, except on *Shabbos.* And we don't go swimming.

In the late afternoon, just before *Tishah B'Av* begins, we have a final meal. We eat some bread dipped in ashes. We also eat a hard egg which is a symbol of mourning.

And we eat these while sitting either on the ground or on a low bench.

Adults do not eat or drink from the evening of *Tishah B'Av* until the following night. We don't wear leather shoes. In synagogues the lights are not all turned on and the beautiful curtains covering the Torah Ark are removed.

On the night of *Tishah B'Av* we read the book of *Eichah* (Lamentations) which mourns over the destruction of the first Temple. And in the evening and morning of *Tishah B'Av*, we say *kinos*, prayers of mourning. In many synagogues a special *kinah* is said in memory of the six million Jews murdered during the Nazi Holocaust.

The *Shabbos* after *Tishah B'Av* is called *Shabbos Nachamu*. The *Haftarah* (Prophets reading) begins with the words "*Nachamu, nachamu ami* — "Be comforted, be comforted My people." It comforts the Jewish people, and tells how G-d will return us to Jerusalem.

Other Fast Days Commemorating the Destruction of the Temple

long with *Tishah B'Av*, there are three other fast days commemorating the destruction of the Temple. On these days adults do not eat or drink. (In Jewish law an adult is any male over the age of thirteen and any female over the age of twelve.) These are not just days of no food nor drink. These are days to think about our sins, to be sorry for the wrongs we have done, and to resolve to follow G-d's laws more carefully in the future.

Tzom Gedalyah

This fast day comes right after *Rosh Hashanah* on the third day of *Tishrei.* It begins in the morning, before sunrise, and ends in the evening, after dark. Adults fast in memory of Gedalyah ben Achikam.

Over two thousand years ago the First Temple was destroyed by Nebuchadnezzar, the King of Babylonia. Most Jews were taken to Babylon. But some remained in the Land of Israel. Nebuchadnezzar appointed Gedalyah to be the governor of those who remained. As long as there were still Jews in the Land, the people had hope. But a treacherous Jew, who was an agent of the King of Ammon, poisoned Gedalyah. When that happened, the remaining Jews in the Land of Israel became frightened and fled to Egypt. After the killing of Gedalyah our people no longer lived in our land.

Asarah B'Teves

It was on the tenth of *Teves* that the soldiers of King Nebuchadnezzar, surrounded Jerusalem. No one could enter the city and no one could leave. No food or water came into Jerusalem. The people starved. It was the beginning of the destruction of the First Temple. Adults fast to remember that horrible time.

❧ Shivah Asar B'Tammuz

The seventeenth day of *Tammuz* is a fast day. We remember many terrible happenings of that date.

Moses came down from *Har Sinai* forty days after G-d had given the Torah. He was holding the Tablets of the Ten Commandments. Moses saw the Jews dancing around a golden calf. He threw down the Tablets he was holding and broke them. It was the seventeenth day of *Tammuz.*

During the time of the First Temple, King Nebuchadnezzar and his army besieged Jerusalem, but the Jews continued to do the service in the Temple. On the seventeeth of *Tammuz,* the daily sacrifices at the Temple stopped. There were no longer any sheep for the offerings. Three weeks later, on the ninth of *Av,* the First Temple was destroyed.

During the time of the Second Temple, it was on the seventeenth of *Tammuz* that the Romans led by the wicked Titus broke through the walls of Jerusalem. Three weeks later, on the ninth of *Av,* the Second Temple was destroyed.

The seventeenth of *Tammuz* is the beginning of a three week period of mourning for the First and Second Temples which were destroyed.

Rosh Chodesh

osh Chodesh marks the beginning of a Jewish month. Some months begin with one day of *Rosh Chodesh,* others with two. The days of *Rosh Chodesh* are set by the phases of the moon.

Toward the end of a Jewish month, we see less and less of the moon, until we cannot see it at all. The next month, the "New Moon", begins when we can see the moon again.

In the Land of Israel during the time of the Temple, people watched eagerly for the new moon. When it was seen, the *Sanhedrin* declared the beginning of a new month, *Rosh Chodesh.*

At first, large fires were lit on the tops of mountains

[47]